The Car Trip

by Helen Oxenbury

Dial Books for Young Readers

E. P. Dutton, Inc. New York

One day we went for a ride.
We took along some sandwiches.

I made believe I was a lion.
"How can Daddy drive properly
with all that noise?" Mommy said.

I went with Daddy to pay for the gas.
"Can I please have some candy?" I said.

At lunchtime we went to a cafeteria.
I only wanted ice cream.

"Take a nap now," Mommy said.
"We won't be home till late."
"I have to go to the bathroom," I said.

"I think it's going to rain,"
 Mommy said.
"I feel sick," I said.
"Quick! Stop!" Mommy shouted.

We cleaned up the car.
Then it wouldn't start again.
Daddy tried and tried,
but nothing happened.
"Call a garage for help!" he said.

A truck towed us home.
I got to sit next to the driver.
"Today was the best car trip ever!"
I told my friends.